THE MOLD FARMER

Rick Claypool

Six Gallery Press

THE MOLD FARMER

1

I'M HALF-BURIED IN A PILE of what used to be the ceiling. My legs are pinned under a refrigerator. My right foot, crushed. I stink of urine.

I try to get up but I can't. Two mechanoids are holding me down. They won't let me sit up. They won't let me move.

Mr. Weckett stands over me. He's the one who owns the mold farm. He's my boss. I'd thought of him as a friend. Now I know he was never my friend.

Weckett's face is clenched. In one arm he cradles a metal bowl. When he crouches down, syrupy yellow stuff slops out of the bowl onto his sleeve. He seems not to notice.

"No," I say. "Please. Just help me out of here. Just let me go."

Weckett's eyes meet mine. "There are rules that must be followed," he says, shaking his head. "Debts that must be paid." A segmented appendage reaches out from the bowl. The appendage ends in a curved claw. It scrapes along the front of his coveralls. "You could ruin me," he says, standing up and stepping back. The room's walls, floor, and the remains of the ceiling are thick with a marbled mix of pink, black, yellow, and gray mold. "All of this will go to waste."

"I'm sorry," I say. "I didn't think..."

"Whether you're sorry or not doesn't matter," he says. "Your lies—and your failure to control your," he hesitates, "your *leakage* mean this entire house must be destroyed. So you're going to pay me back. You're going to have to work off your debt. You'll work for me for the rest of your life. Assuming you live."

"Please," I say. The shreds of my ruined foot send sharp pulses to my skull. I wish I could just dissolve in the blood and piss and rain dampening everything around me.

Weckett dips his free hand into the bowl and scoops out the thing. Yellow fluid drips from his fingers and runs down his sleeve. The thing is horrible. A lump of blue-gray flesh covered in nostril-like openings. A hygienic void.

The openings pucker and flare. The void's single appendage reaches blindly. It is feeling for something alive to hook onto, to pull itself inside of.

"I don't have a choice," Weckett says.

"Of course you have a choice," is what I want to say. But, looking at the thing in his hand, I am so overcome with fear that I throw up, mostly on myself.

I gasp for breath.

The thing's appendage whips into my open mouth.

It anchors its claw between my teeth.

It starts pulling itself in.

One of the mechanoids moves away. The other binds my wrists. The edges of its metal hands cut into my skin. The mechanoid that moved away clamps its hands on either side of my head. I can tell from the pressure those cold metal fingers exert that it easily could crush my skull if Weckett asked. The hands squeeze until I scream.

The hygienic void pulls itself toward my face. It presses against my nose and lips until my teeth are cutting into the inside of my mouth. I resist but it's too strong. It forces my jaw open wider than it should. It's as if the bottom half of my face is unhinging. My screams are muffled. I feel the nostril-like openings suck against my tongue, the insides of my cheeks, the back of my throat.

I gag and gag and gag until my gagging feels like I might throw up the inside of my head. And then I gag some more.

2

MY MOTHER WAS A MURDERER.

She hated being a murderer, but there were powerful people who were willing to pay to have other people eliminated, and mom had a family, so she did what she thought she had to do so we could survive.

I don't judge her. I judge dad. He murdered her. I never found out why, but she killed a lot of people so there were plenty who wanted revenge and were willing to pay for it. It might have been for some other reason, but I always assumed it was just money.

Dad had a shard problem, which would have made him easy to manipulate. Mom was so much stronger and faster than dad, I don't know how he pulled it off. It's not something I like to think about so I haven't tried very hard to figure it out.

I was very young when all this happened, just barely beginning to grow random wisps of hair on my chin. A day or two after the murder, my sister told me she was going to run away to the mountains. I didn't want to run to the mountains. But then sooner than I expected, she was gone. I didn't want to be alone with dad either so on the next day I left too.

I found shelter under an old bridge. The bridge, a steel and concrete structure spanning what once was a road, was situated on the outskirts of a tuber farm. Over time I dug myself a burrow in the dirt under one side of the bridge. The burrow made for a reasonable shelter for storing stolen tubers and hiding when the temperature dropped. During that summer and fall I lived completely alone and spoke to no one. Under the bridge was more of a home for me than my true home ever had been. I felt truly and terrifyingly free.

When the darkest part of winter came, I found that despite my efforts to keep my existence secret, the people who farmed the tubers knew about me. One bitterly cold day I woke up to find a small bag of tubers, wood for my fire, and a pile of dry blankets at the mouth of my burrow. These gifts started to appear with some regularity.

The months passed into spring and I wondered what I should do. Taking advantage of the tuber farmers' charity embarrassed me. I felt I had only two choices: thank the farmers in person by offering to work for them, or put as much distance as possible between myself and the people I was indebted to by leaving this place forever.

Before I could decide, I found my burrow suddenly occupied by a slug pig.

I'd been hunting rats in a garbage heap some five miles away. After killing a whole sackful, I'd wash them in a stream and sort out any visibly diseased ones, then carry my kills back to skin and boil.

Back under the bridge, I knew right away something was wrong. The heavy, flat rock I used as the door do my burrow was askew and loose piles of dirt surrounded the opening. I leaned over the hole and looked down. Darkness was all I could see. I took a rat out of my sack and dropped it in. When the rat hit the ground, the slug pig pounced. It swallowed the rat whole, then looked up at me.

The slug pig was a vile, blunt-faced thing. The front of its huge head was smeared with eyes and other sensory organs—nostrils, feelers, earlike whorls and inexplicable protrusions—all surrounding the sphincter of its mouth.

Slug pigs had come with the mask wearers, the nglaeylyaethm, and like the beings that brought them, all that could be done was to adapt and accommodate to their presence. I didn't have a weapon that could hurt it. If I angered it, it could trample me to death without much effort.

Reluctantly, I sought the tuber farmers' help.

The slug pig's meat was poisonous and its hide would flake uselessly away like the skin of an onion after it was dead, so offering to let them keep the killed creature would be useless. I decided I would offer to work on the farm in exchange for their help killing the slug pig.

I approached the tuber farmers' fire pit. An elder was sitting nearby, meditating near a group of four or five children giggling in the mud. The elder was shirtless and wore his gray hair in long, twisted braids. I stood by the smoldering pit until the elder opened his eyes. "You're the boy who lives under the overpass," he said.

Being recognized by this man I'd never seen before surprised me. He looked at me calmly and directly. It was unsettling. It reminded me how my mother used to look at me, her eyes full of love and worry. "My name is Thorner," I said, and told him about the slug pig and that I could help on the farm in exchange for help. Without a moment's thought, he shook his head, making his braids sway. "No," he said. "If you work here, you can stay here. Come with me." He stood up, introduced himself as Girban, and told me to follow him.

Girban took me down a small grassy slope. At the bottom, at the edge of a forest of fallen trees, was the largest tent I'd ever seen. What it was, I realized, was a whole network of interconnected tents. On one end was a huge, dome-shaped section I guessed could easily hold 30 or 40 people at a time. I could see that other parts of the tent spiraled outward from the dome. The overall shape made me think of a bunch of snails huddled together under a rock.

"Pondai!" he called, and waited. Then, louder, "Pondai!"

A woman came out of the structure and ran toward us. She was probably in her 20s. She was tall and her hair was short and she had a look in her eyes like she resented being summoned like that. I noticed her hands and Girban's hands were stained gray.

"How is our mask wearer husk supply? Do we have enough extra to make space for Thorner here?"

She glanced at me, then back at Girban. "We have enough," she said.

"Then take Thorner here and show him how to make himself a room."

Pondai nodded and turned back toward the immense tent. I ran after her. She matter-of-factly showed me where the shedded nglaeylyaethm husks were kept and how and where I should stitch a section for myself onto the big tent. Then she handed me a rough cake of soap. "With everyone living close together like this, it's better not to stink," she said.

I washed myself in a cold shower rigged up at the edge of the farm, then got to work setting up my section of tent. The mask wearer husks were a pain to work with. They were hard and brittle in some places and rubbery and stretchy in others. Networks of capillaries were visible in their brownish gray surfaces if you held them up to the light.

I got to work, intending to finish as fast as I could. My work was rushed, my stitching sloppy. I didn't care. In that moment I desperately wanted to be a member of this community, and the sooner I assembled a place to sleep, the sooner it would be official. I stabbed my fingers with the sewing needle Pondai gave me over and over again. I bled on the thread that was supposed to hold my space together, and if my stitching was crooked or failed to connect properly with other sections of my structure-in-progress or the pre-existing structure, I told myself it didn't matter.

Pondai came to check on my progress. She looked, then shook her head. "Tear it down," she said. "And start over."

I was partway through my second attempt when a girl about my age brought me some dumplings stuffed with mashed tubers. Her hands were gray too. She introduced herself as Shully while I was already stuffing my face. She inspected my stitchwork. "You know you're going to have to start over again *again*," she said.

I groaned and fell over dramatically. Shully giggled. Her smile was magic. She had long braided hair and brown eyes that made me feel so completely seen, it was simultaneously liberating and embarrassing.

Shully explained to me slowly and painstakingly the things about proper tentmaking that just seemed like common sense to others in her community. She told me to sew smaller, tighter stitches to keep out mosquitoes and other crawling, biting things. She helped me stitch my section on straight, which she reminded me was especially important because if mine was crooked, any sections that others built that were connected to mine also would be crooked. And when I was nearly finished, she stopped me from opening an entrance slit on the wrong side of the tent—the correct way, she showed me, was to have it open into the big tent, where it was attached to a common hallway inside.

Pondai didn't even stop to inspect this final attempt at tent making. When she walked past on the way to do something else, she simply said, "Looks alright, Thorner," and continued toward more important things.

3

I DIDN'T REALIZE AT THE TIME that Pondai and Shully were sisters, both Girban's daughters.

Six or seven families made up the entire tuber farming community. Girban was the nominal leader because he originally started the farm. But he didn't really lead anything besides the work of farming and preserving the tubers they lived on. Which was an important thing, but probably not the most important thing.

Pondai and Shully's mother had died in one of the many epidemics that decimated what was left of the human population every few years. She died a long time ago, or so it seemed from Girban and his daughters' matter-of-fact attitude about her absence.

Pondai was the real leader. She organized the meetings where the adults gathered to plan ways to meet everyone's needs, to make sure there was enough food, to take care of the children, to support the sick and injured, to thwart outside threats. When people had problems, it was Pondai they went to for help.

After I first arrived, there was a big meeting where I was introduced as a new member of the community. During that meeting, there was a heated debate over whether organizing a group to go out and kill the slug pig that took over my burrow was worth the risk. I don't remember what the group's official decision was, but there were some older kids who decided over the objections of their parents that they would hunt it down and kill it themselves.

During the next meeting, there was another heated debate, this time about who was to blame after one of these older kids lost a foot when the wounded slug pig chomped it off during its death throes.

I found the meetings confusing and overwhelming. There was never any violence but there almost always was shouting. After what had happened to my parents, I had a hard time handling my fear that the heated arguments that occasionally flared up would lead to people killing each other. Usually I sat out the meetings. Instead, I volunteered to look after the little kids, who were overwhelming in n way but far less frightening than the adults, for

t part.

Seasons passed. Very little changed. The community thrived.

Then one summer, slug pigs overran the tuber crop.

There must have been thousands of them lumbering and rooting around.

They devoured everything. Girban led teams of hunters out shooting as many as they could, but there were too many. The slug pigs didn't even run, and did not hesitate to cannibalize the fallen slug pigs the hunters killed.

Winter that year was hard. To supplement the poor tuber crop, families ventured off seeking to trade work or goods for food. Some never came back.

I helped Shully make tents for the departing families. Making tents from shedded nglaeylyaethm husks was staining my hands gray too. When Shully noticed, she took one of my hands in both of hers and studied it closely. She kissed my fingertips. I froze, uncertain what was happening and afraid if I said or did anything she might stop. She brought my calloused palm up to her cheek.

We made a secret tent for ourselves to sneak away to when we wanted to be alone.

The slug pigs overran the tuber crop again the next year. And the next.

The community dissolved.

Girban gave up. For days he would just lie inside his tent until some impulse or another forced him out. Shully and I avoided him.

Not Pondai. Pondai was responsible for our survival. She hunted rabbits and caught fish and when there was nothing larger she gathered beetles and grubs. She put plants in front of us she insisted were edible. I don't think she was always right but we always helped her gather what we could, and we always ate what we had to eat. And we survived.

I know there were times when Pondai tried to be there for her father, when she was gentle and patient with him. She knew sadness had seeped deep in his bones after the collapse of everything he ever worked for, the end of the community he created. She knew he was nursing wounds that would never fully heal.

But eventually her patience wore out. She was hungry and angry and terrified too.

She needed him to help. He wasn't helping. She let him know.

Shully and I were blowing on coals, trying to reignite a fire under a shallow pot of water we were trying to boil. We were going to make soup from some grackle eggs Pondai found. The ground was damp and so were the sticks we used for kindling.

Girban came out of his tent and stood there by the fire with us, not saying anything and watching the water not boil.

Pondai stalked out from the edge of the woods with weeds in her fists. She threw the weeds into the pot, then turned so her face was inches from Girban's. "So you're hungry now, old man?" she shoved him. He stumbled backward and fell. He was weak. I thought I caught a quick look of shock on her face—shock that Girban fell so easily, and maybe an instant of regret for losing her temper. She glanced at us, said, "Keep blowing," then turned back to Girban. Her face hardened again. "You want to eat? Help. You don't want to help? Fine. But you can crawl right back to your tent."

Weeping, he started crawling back to his tent.

After a minute or so his thin limbs gave out and he stopped crawling. Pondai ran to his side. I thought she was going to help him. But something had been unleashed in her, a rage she must have been suppressing for a long time. "I said crawl!" she shouted. When he didn't move, she yelled "Crawl!" again and kicked him in the ribs. He fell sideways and groaned. Then she looked back at Shully and me. "I said keep blowing!"

Shully and I hardly ate any of the soup that night. We took our leftovers to Girban after dark. I don't know if he got to eat any. Pondai kicked over the soup pot outside Girban's tent when she saw it in the morning.

This was the state we were in when the pet store owner's caravan arrived.

It was midday when the ramshackle cart pulled by four harnessed slug pigs trundled down into our valley.

Pondai was elsewhere, trying to barter food in exchange for gloves, hats, and small tents Shully and I had made from salvaged sections of what once was the community's enormous tent.

Girban was still in his tent, asleep or immobilized by despair.

Shully and I were at the pond, trying to catch toads now that they'd laid their eggs. We heard the noise and stood to gawk at the stranger arriving in his strange mode of conveyance. Harnessed slug pigs were something I'd never seen before.

The man pulled the reins, halting the slug pigs and his caravan, and leapt down. He was small and clean-shaven and the clothes he wore looked extraordinarily clean and close-fitting.

"Hello!" he shouted in a sharp voice and introduced himself as Olmer. "You kids look hungry," he said, eyeing our emaciated bodies. "Are you all by yourselves here? Are you alone?"

In response, we stared at him blankly, stole a quick glance at each other, then started running.

"Wait!" he shouted, "Wait, wait, wait!" We stopped. The pond was between us and Olmer now. We exchanged glances again. "I don't mean any harm," Olmer continued, smiling as he spoke. "I just thought you might be interested in some of the delicious food I brought to share. And if you're not alone, if you have more people with you than just each other, then I'll just need to bring out more food. Do you understand? I don't mean any harm."

"They're not alone," said Girban, his voice sounding raspy and hollow. Neither Shully and I nor Olmer must have noticed him come out of his tent. He stood between Olmer and us now, and seemed stronger than he had for some time.

"Indeed they are not!" said Olmer. He walked up to Girban and looked him over. If he stood on his toes, the top of his head wouldn't have reached Girban's shoulder. He poked Girban in the ribs. "I'd be happy to share some of the delicious food I brought with you too. Wait right here."

Girban had a look on his face like he'd crush Olmer's head if he had the strength.

Olmer hurried back to his caravan. Soon he returned with a stack of pots, which he arranged on a white blanket he laid out. He opened the pots, revealing a variety of warm, meaty stews inside. He handed us spoons. "Enjoy," he said. "Please, enjoy."

Now Girban, Shully, and I all exchanged looks. Of course we were suspicious. Strangers didn't arrive out of nowhere offering free food for nothing. But we were starving. And after about ten seconds, Girban visibly relaxed and gestured for us to come with him toward the food. "Alright, Olmer," he said. "Thank you for the feast."

The food was like nothing I'd ever had before or since. There was a green stew and a red stew and an orange stew and a yellow stew. Some were creamy and some were spicy. Some had tender chunks of meat, some had crunchy vegetables, some had chewy grains. And any time it seemed like any of the particularly tasty pots were almost empty, Olmer brought more.

After we were good and full, Olmer brought us tiny drinks with so much alcohol they stung our lips and numbed our tongues. "And now that everyone is full," Olmer said, "it is time for us to talk business." He smiled, and there was something off about his smile. "If any of you would like to come with me, I can make it so none of you will go hungry ever again. I can make it so you can enjoy meals like this whenever you want."

"Save your speech," said Girban. "I'll go with you."

Olmer's grin widened. "Wonderful!" he said. "Though if I can persuade two of you, I am prepared to be twice as generous, you see— "

"Stop talking," said Girban. "Or I won't go with you. I know what you are. I know what you do."

Olmer nodded. "Of course. I'll just draw up the paperwork," he said. He gathered the pots in his blanket and carried them back to the caravan.

"Dad," said Shully, "what are you doing?"

"Helping." He closed his eyes and sighed deeply.

"I don't understand," said Shully.

"Good," he said. "It's better that way."

I didn't understand either.

I assumed Girban had some kind of plan.

I assumed he knew best.

I assumed things would work out.

Olmer returned with a heavy canvas hoisted over his shoulder. He dropped the bag in front of Shully and me. "This should be fair," he said.

Girban opened the sack. He pulled out a roll of tokens about as long as his forearm. The tokens were held together with plastic. "Each of these rolls is five hundred?" Olmer nodded. Girban counted the rest. "Alright. This will do," he said.

"I'll wait for you at the cart," said Olmer.

Girban knelt down in front of Shully. "This is for the best," he said. There was no sign of emotion in his face. "Tell your sister I helped the only way I knew how. Tell her I'm sorry."

Shully nodded. Her eyes started tearing up. "I still don't understand."

Girban hugged her. "We don't always understand everything we have to struggle through," he said. "We just have to struggle through. Now you take good care of Thorner, alright?" She nodded. "And you take good care of my little girl, you hear me Thorner?" I nodded.

Then Girban walked over and climbed into Olmer's caravan, and the slug pigs pulled them away.

Night seemed to fall suddenly.

Shully and I whispered attempts to explain to each other what we thought had happened. Our best guess was that Olmer had taken Girban far away to do some kind of work for him. "Maybe growing things," I said. "Maybe building something."

"Maybe he'll be training slug pigs," suggested Shully. "He'd hate that."

"Imagine slug pigs that do tricks," I said, and started listing off strange and silly things to make a slug pig do.

We chuckled softly at the thought of dancing slug pigs and fell asleep.

"WAKE UP, YOU TWO," said Pondai, her head poking into our tent. "Dad is missing."

"We know," I said, yawning and stretching. "He left with a man who came yesterday. And they left us this." I smacked the sack of tokens, which we'd dragged into our tent.

Pondai grabbed the sack with both hands and hauled it out of the tent. She opened it and looked inside. As she looked, I got up and stood next to her. Shully followed close behind.

Pondai turned her face toward mine, her bloodshot eyes brimming with fury. She slapped me hard, then reached for Shully. She grabbed Shully's arm and pulled her in front of me and pointed to the sack. "What is this?"

"The man gave it to us," Shully said meekly. "I told

Dad I didn't understand. He didn't explain. All he said was that he was helping. He said to tell you he's sorry."

Pondai slapped Shully.

I got up and charged at Pondai.

She knocked me back down without much effort.

"You sold him," said Pondai. "Do you understand?"

Tears were glistening in the corners of Shully's eyes but her jaw was set. She shook her head.

"That man bought our father from you, sister," Pondai hissed. "He bought him from you, and now he'll sell him to the mask wearers. We will never see him again. That man was a pet store owner. Understand?"

Pondai didn't wait for a response. She took the sack of tokens and heaved it into a hand cart. "Do you know which way they went?"

I told her they were in a caravan pulled by slug pigs and I pointed in the direction I thought they went. Shully said nothing.

"Stay here," said Pondai, "I'm going to buy him back."

She dragged the cart over the hill in the direction I said she should go.

5

Days passed. Then weeks. Then months.

Eventually Shully and I agreed neither her sister nor her father were coming back.

And we agreed we had to leave.

We carried away as much tentmaking material as we could and set off for a different community where no one knew us.

It wasn't easy but there was a period of time when we managed to survive somewhat comfortably.

OUR GIRL, PIXA, was born on a moonless night.

I remember Shully suddenly sitting up and repeating over and over, "It's coming, it's coming." I fumbled with blankets, trying to figure out the best way to arrange them around her. For some reason the blankets seemed very important at the time. Her forehead was damp and she was shivering. I didn't know what I was doing. I was in a daze. Nothing seemed real.

Retha the midwife arrived and said not to worry, she'd delivered over a thousand babies. She said everything would be fine. She had muscular arms and she took Shully's one leg and I took the other leg and together we put a blanket under her and dragged her screaming out of our tent and toward the communal fire. Retha wanted to make sure she could see what she was doing.

Retha told me to get a pot of water and put it on the fire. She used the boiling water to sterilize her tools, some of which looked alarmingly sharp to me. I couldn't stop looking at those tools and thinking how their purpose was to puncture skin, that they had punctured the skins of countless mothers and babies and now they would be used on Shully and our child. Even as I held Shully's hand as she was pushing and Pixa's wet, hairy head was beginning to emerge, I was worrying about those tools.

After Pixa's birth, Retha used a blade from the pot to sever the cord while Pixa clung weakly to Shully's breast. I couldn't imagine any of the other sharp tools being necessary now. But still I was afraid the tools might have uses beyond the limits of my imagination. Irrationally, I kept expecting Retha to take something else from the pot and try to stab Shully or Pixa with it. She didn't. But I imagined myself stepping forward so I was the one who was stabbed, so Shully and Pixa would be saved.

Retha helped us back inside. In the tent, she sponge-bathed Shully and Pixa. I used some of the still-warm water from Retha's pot of tools to wash our blankets.

I stood watch outside after Retha left.

The encampment where we lived was barely visible

in the firelight. It wasn't much to look at anyway, all hard-packed dirt and rocks and random tufts of brown, stubby plants. A hundred or so tents belonging to other families were spread out around the shallow valley. Ours was one of the larger tents, thanks to our trade, with a central dome and three cone-shaped rooms sticking out of the sides.

That night I worried that maybe our tent was a little too fancy. That a large, well-made tent like ours might attract unwanted attention.

I grew anxious and in response to my anxiety I gave in to the urge I'd been trying to stifle in myself: I started feeling around in my satchel for my last half-dose of shard.

I hadn't yet found the little half-capsule when Stoker, one of the encampment elders, appeared out of the darkness to congratulate me. He was bald and his limbs were lean and ropy. He put his arm around my shoulders and spoke in a hushed tone. "Six months since a newborn has been taken," he said. "I can keep watch for you till sunup, if you like."

I accepted Stoker's offer and decided to save the shard.

In our tent, I lay in bed listening to the rhythm of Shully and Pixa breathing in their sleep. Shully was propped up with a pile of foam-filled bags for pillows. Pixa snored softly on her chest. I tried remembering if I'd seen any desperate-looking shard addicts lingering at the edge of the encampment. I wasn't sure and I cursed myself for not being sure. Strangers always came and went and I'd never paid them much attention. I should have paid attention. There were shard addicts who would take a newborn and then ransom it back to you. In the future, I told myself, I would have to be more alert. In the future, I would have to do better.

Because in that moment I knew if Pixa were taken I would not hesitate to offer everything we had in exchange for her safe return.

I tried reassuring myself. I thought comforting thoughts. I needed sleep. Any minute, Pixa could make us wake up. I told myself to be glad a kind elder was guarding our tent and grateful my own shard habit was under control. I reminded myself giving birth had not hurt Shully and our baby was healthy and our food and water stores would last at least a month, maybe more. Definitely more if our neighbors brought us food, which often happens after a baby arrives and survives.

From outside the tent, I heard the buzz of insects,

the occasional pop from the bonfire, Stoker's friendly whispers of greeting to the odd passer-by. Familiar, comforting sounds that finally lulled me to sleep.

I heard Stoker cry out for help.

I jumped out of bed and picked up my hunting rifle.

I opened the tent flap and saw Stoker twitching on the ground, his throat cut.

I charged outside.

Dozens of crazed shard addicts surrounded our tent. Their eyes were empty holes and their noses were empty holes and their mouths were empty holes, like skulls. Rags cloaked their bodies and in their clawlike hands they carried long blades.

I shot at them.

They kept coming.

Some reached the back of our tent and started hacking into it with their blades, tearing holes they'd use to get inside and kill Shully and steal Pixa.

One by one, I shot them.

But there were too many.

I heard Pixa cry out.

And it was the first time Pixa's wailing woke me.

I was breathing hard. I was shaking. Usually when I woke up like this Shully would put her arms around me and hold me until I stopped shaking.

Waking up like this was something that happened to me sometimes.

I took a deep breath.

Shully and I looked at each other in the glow of the sunlight coming through the wrinkled, veiny material of the tent. It was as if we were able truly to see each other for the first time in a long time.

Stoker's voice called into the tent: "Hey Daddy, someone left some fruit out here for you. Come and get it and I'll be on my way."

In that moment, as Pixa nursed hungrily at Shully's breast and I retrieved the fruit and bread and butter our neighbors had left, it seemed like nothing in the world could shatter our sweaty, crusty, hungry, grimy, smelly familial bliss.

7

NILDA OPENED A SMALL BAG and sniffed, then made a face like she was going to puke.

She shoved the bag back under the pile of tents in my cart. She felt around until she found another small bag and pulled it out, carefully holding it close to herself, keeping it hidden. She opened it and sniffed, and made the face again. "They're rotten, Thorner," she said, shoving the bag back under the pile. "Way more rotten than usual." She pulled the hood of her cloak over her head. "How much?"

"Three hundred tokens." Normally I would have asked for 400. She was right about the nglaeylyaethm organs. They were rotten. And as more and more vendors were arriving around me to set up shop, I was increasingly anxious to complete our illicit transaction.

"I'll give you half that."

I shook my head. "Two hundred?" I was begging. Nilda was my only customer for the organs, an essential ingredient for making shard. She knew I had to get rid of them. And she knew I trusted her.

"One fifty," she insisted. "You know I'm already being generous."

"Alright,' I said. "Throw in four doses and we have a deal." I was getting nervous. I'd been sloppy, I'd pulled my cart too close to the nglaeylaethm section of the market, and now I saw Jolm Hunter setting up his pet store directly across from me. If I was going to stomach the screams I'd hear all day, I was going to need at least a half-dose right away. And I didn't want to even think about what might happen if Nilda didn't buy the organs.

"I'll give you two."

"That won't last me a week."

"Not my problem," Nilda smirked.

Jolm yelled for me in his booming voice. "Tenter! Hey, Thorner Tenter! Come here."

I nodded at Nilda. She slipped me the coins and doses in powder-filled capsules. I reached under the pile of tents on my cart and used my arm to push twenty dumpling-sized bags hidden underneath into the large satchel she carried.

Jolm stepped up behind her. He stood a full head taller than her and was almost twice as wide. His imposing body made it so Nilda couldn't slip away without brushing against his body as she squeezed past. "Hey Thorner, you smell spaghetti cooking?" he teased as she slumped down and narrowed her shoulders to push through. She was doing her best not to actually acknowledge Jolm's presence. "Suddenly I'm craving a big bowl of noodles."

I wanted to tell Jolm to leave Nilda alone, but I didn't. For the whole day I was going to be stuck across from Jolm and the other vendors set up all around him, and all of their customers were going to be nglaeylyaethm. "You're the *noodle server*," is what I wanted to say. I gritted my teeth. Anyway, it's a contested insult. Sometimes it's used against people like me and Nilda, whose business is selling nglaeylyaethm parts. Sometimes it's used against people like Jolm, whose business caters to nglaeylyaethm customers.

As Nilda hurried away, Jolm made a loud slurping noise at her with his lips. Then he turned to me, smiling stupidly. "Got a job for you."

"You need a tent?" I said, retrieving a small display

tent from my cart. I held it up for him to inspect.

"Is that what you sold her in those little bags? A tent?"

"Sutures," I confidently lied, shifting into salesman mode. "If you need sutures or just about anything else for repairing your nglaeylyaethm-husk tent, I have it here. What do you need?"

"I need a custom job," he said. "I need twenty, no, thirty bags. They should be just big enough to hold a person, with an opening on top for the head to poke out, and I should be able to tighten the opening around the person's neck. Do you understand?"

I understood and I didn't want to do it. I wanted to refuse. After what had happened to her father, Shully would hate it. I would hate it.

But with Pixa now two years old and growing hungrier every day, we needed the tokens.

I popped open the miniature display tent and placed it on the ground. "I'll have to speak with my partner. She makes the tents," I said. "There's a backlog of custom jobs we still have to finish," I lied again. "She'll know what's possible."

The smile on Jolm's round face widened. "Thanks,

Thorner," he said. "Hope you can have something for me soon. I can give you twenty tokens a bag. These canvas bags I always use, they'll last a little longer, but they smell. I need something new. I'm sure noodle skin will contain the smell better than canvas."

I understood why Jolm wanted to cover the smell. Even from across the path I occasionally caught a whiff of the foulness inside his caravan. He was probably right about nglaeylyaethm skin containing the smell better than canvas. Still, it would do nothing to silence the wailing of his wares.

The sound of vendors shouting nearby interrupted my chat with Jolm. The shouts were unmistakable pleas for attention—claims about the high quality or low-cost quantity of strange commodities. Two nglaeylyaethm were now coming toward us down the dirt path between vendors and the vendors were desperately trying to make a sale.

Jolm hurried back to his stall. I hid behind my cart and tent display.

Nglaeylyaethm look like horse-sized masses of rust-colored tentacles. A gaunt, slow-moving person walked close beside the larger of the two. As they came nearer, I could distinguish the knotted clusters of trunk-like tendrils that made up the creatures' main bodies from the numerous whiplike tentacles sprouting from this central mass. They used these smaller tentacles like hands and fingers, to manipulate small objects. Their undersides were covered in countless stubby, fingerlike extensions that they walked on.

The end of one of the larger one's tentacles was buried in the back of the gaunt person's head.

The two nglaeylyaethm stopped when they arrived at Jolm's stall. Their bodies gave off a smell like ozone and sulphur.

Nglaeylyaethm always wear a vaguely human-looking rubber mask on one of their thicker tentacles. The masks look like whoever among the nglaeylyaethm makes them hasn't quite figured out the precise arrangement of features that make up a human face. When they interact with a human, they always make sure the mask is facing the human's face. There is no sign of eyes or any other sensory organ behind the mask.

As far as I can tell, they can't perceive the world around them on their own. That's what their pets are for.

I hid from the mask wearers because I didn't want them to notice my gray-stained hands. The stains would give me away as someone who works with nglaeylyaethm flesh. Of course, being a tenter, I'd have a good excuse, since our tents are made from the discarded skin they leave behind after molting. But I knew the stains would offend the nglaeylyaethm, and likely invite attention from the patrolling para-sights, so it would be for the best if I avoided being noticed. There's a lot that can go wrong for someone who winds up answering questions while looking at the curled-up grublike things inhabiting the eye sockets of those agents of the nglaeylyaethm.

Now Jolm was speaking to the larger mask wearer's pet. He gestured toward the inside of his caravan. The pet said something to Jolm, who nodded his head, then disappeared inside. A moment later he returned dragging a large, filthy sack with both hands. A man's head with wild, greasy hair and a wiry beard stuck out of the top. Both of the nglaeylyaethm proceeded to touch the man's face with their tentacles. Then the pet stepped forward and gave the man in the sack a shove. The man, who must have been kneeling on his knees inside the sack, fell sideways and landed in the dirt with a dull thud. The pet picked the person back up. Then Jolm and the pet talked a little bit more.

The pet finally handed Jolm a small bag of tokens,

which Jolm counted. After Jolm finished counting, he helped the pet hold down the man in the sack while the smaller mask wearer forced a tentacle into the back of his head.

The man was screaming the whole time this was happening.

After the mask wearers moved on, I came out of hiding. I unfolded a chair and took a seat beside my display tent. When I looked at Jolm, he wiggled his arms over his head in a way I knew he was making fun of the nglaeylyaethm.

I didn't think it was funny. I laughed anyway.

8

"We'll take the job," I said.

Jolm took one of my gray hands in his sweaty fist and shook. "Wonderful," he said, yellow teeth sticking out of his grin. "Excellent."

When I first mentioned the job to Shully, we decided right away we'd never work for Jolm. "He's on *their* side," Shully had said. "He might as well not even be human."

Then I had an idea. "What if we took the job, but stitched the sacks together just a *little* too loosely? Not so loose that Jolm would notice right away. Like, just loose enough so the captives can work holes into them after a few days. Just loose enough that they can escape, but we come out looking like we had made an honest mistake?"

"Yes!" Shully said.

Shully stitched tricks into the sacks, weak seams and loose threads that everyday shifts and struggles would eventually undo.

A week after we sold Jolm the sacks, the para-sights came for us.

They appeared in the pinkish morning light.

They surrounded our tent and tore it down.

They dragged us out and interrogated us by the dying bonfire. Pixa clung to me, sobbing quietly.

One para-sight jabbed his egg gun into my stomach and growled a litany of anti-nglaeylyaethm accusations at me. The grublike parasite living in his face in place of one of his eyes squirmed in its socket, transmitting my every word to the para-sights' masters' crystal city in the sky.

I denied everything. Shully denied everything. Even Pixa, who surely had heard, even if she did not entirely understand, our conspiratorial conversations, said nothing of use to our interrogators.

And then, suddenly, the para-sights were no longer holding the egg guns. The three of us were holding the egg guns, even Pixa. We were pointing them at the para-sights, threatening to shoot them and taunting them with our predictions about the otherworldly things that would hatch from the egg-bullets once embedded in a victim's flesh.

Our neighbors appeared. Everyone who lived in our encampment joined us and surrounded the para-sights. They carried crude weapons, sticks and spears and parts of broken things. Their hidden fury had been unleashed. The para-sights didn't stand a chance.

We escaped and found the encampment where Nilda lived, a faraway place the nglaeylyaethm and their agents always avoided because of the atomic weapons the elders possessed. Our entire encampment followed.

The nglaeylyaethm knew from experience we humans were capable of destroying ourselves if we thought doing so was the only way to retaliate against our enemies. We'd done it before and we could do it again. They left us alone.

I become a shard lord. I had more shard than I could ever want, and Pixa's hands were never stained gray like her father's and mother's, she didn't have to survive by making tents out of the nglaeylyaethm's shedded skin.

And then I was awake.

Sheets of rain poured on the tent above me. Everything was damp and dark.

That was when the children came into our tent.

The girl was about ten, the boy maybe six. Their clothes were soaked and their faces were smeared with mud and what looked like dried blood.

I put some tubers into the embers of what had been the small fire in the center of our tent while Shully peeled the wet clothes off their shivering limbs and gave them wool blankets. The noise woke Pixa, who crawled out of her cot and trotted to my side. She half-hid herself behind my leg and stared at the newcomers.

The children sat shivering and staring into the glowing embers. Several minutes passed before either said a word. They didn't have to say anything. Despite not having seen them for years, I knew who they were. And I knew they would not have come unless something terrible had happened.

The girl's name was Uli. She spoke first. "Osna is dead."

The news of the death of my sister—their mother— did not surprise me.

I took Shully looking for her with me after we'd given up waiting for Pondai and Girban. We found her and then almost immediately decided to leave her. She'd let herself be hired by a mountain warlord to spy on a valley warlord. She'd insinuated herself among the valley warlord's advisors and reported everything she could to enemy agents. She enjoyed a great deal of wealth and comfort from both warlords but it did not make up for the obvious precarity of her situation. I told Shully I thought she'd wake up one day with her throat slit and if we stuck around our fate almost certainly would be the same.

I was surprised the children got away.

Uli's eyes shifted back and forth between Shully and me. Her gaze was hard.

Seeking help from our family meant joining us and joining us meant a significant reduction of her social status. She was used to life as a member of her powerful mother's household. Warlord's food stocks, mountain spring water, servants whose lot probably seemed better than ours. Adapting to a tenter's life would not come easy for her.

Kolb let out a scream when his sister mentioned their mother's death. The scream might have been the word "no" or might simply have been a kind of pained animal cry. He was a sad, feral creature. He overflowed with rage. Directing his energies toward productive ends would not be easy.

Nevertheless, the children had arrived at our three-person tent. Shully and I were obligated to take them in.

The children ate two tubers each, then fell asleep side by side on the dirt floor. I returned Pixa to her cot, then joined Shully in our bed. We listened to Pixa snoring and held each other. In whispers we shared our fears about what we would have to do to take care of Uli and Kolb. The broken children frightened us in ways we didn't entirely understand. Their arrival meant the end of our lives' relative simplicity. We mourned its loss and tried to convince each other our fears were unfounded.

Inwardly I cursed my dead sister. I envied her in a way. I thought about what it might be like if I were dead too. The thought helped me sleep.

9

THE FOOD AND WATER STORES that recently seemed more than adequate for our small family suddenly were not enough.

Uli and Kolb rapidly depleted what food we had, even as Shully and I took care to consume less. In five days, we'd gone through supplies I expected before the children arrived to last more than a month.

If we didn't so something, we were going to starve.

Shully and I were hesitant at first to adopt any strategy that was much different from what we'd already been doing. What we'd already been doing mostly had worked, and it had worked for us for what felt like a long time.

We resolved to teach Uli and Kolb the tenting trade. If we increased the number of tents we could make, we figured the children would absorb the extra costs they added to our family.

The plan was doomed from the start.

I started one sunny day by showing Uli how to scavenge for mask wearer husks. Shully meanwhile volunteered to use our last remaining husk to show Kolb how to stitch. Teaching Kolb while looking after Pixa, Shully insisted, would be no trouble at all.

We searched all around my favorite picking grounds. They were weedy fields and rocky hills below where one of the nglaeylyaethm's crystal cities would float by in the sky.

If you see one of their cities in the sky, I explained to Uli, then you will find their garbage on the ground. And that was what we were looking for—the used-up skin those beings dropped from their cities, sometimes in large quantities.

We had bad luck. She would run ahead of me, energetically scouting for the raw material we needed, and over and over again, find nothing. After several hours of this I started having doubts about our plan. The extra capacity for tentmaking the children provided would not necessarily be matched by the availability of husks.

I wondered if pursuing our plan would force us to buy husks at market from other pickers. And if we were forced to buy husks, we would have to raise prices. And we'd have to increase the number of tents I usually sold.

We would have to do business with Jolm. We would have no choice.

Feeling defeated, I slumped down to rest at the foot of an enormous rotting oak. Uli helped me make a fire. If she shared my frustration, she hid it well. She waded up to her knees in greenish creek water, flipping rocks to catch crayfish and insect larva. We used sharp sticks to skewer and cook what she caught.

Not wanting to return empty handed, I took Uli to a broken down cabin where I remembered seeing mask wearer remains that I'd previously dismissed as too small, too inaccessible, and too decayed to be useful.

The road to the cabin crossed over a low hill. Beside the hill was a valley and beside that was another hill covered in acres and acres of houses. "Hard to believe people used to live in buildings like that," I said to Uli. She already was aware of what they were, how they'd been used, how they were used now. But I was feeling frustrated and wanted to talk about nothing and she seemed not to mind listening to me ramble. I rambled on, "Hard to believe it's been a hundred years since anyone lived in a house. A hundred years! I wonder what it was like."

"Not the best time to be a tent maker, I bet," Uli said.

"Maybe they were always full of mold," I said. "Maybe they weren't great for living in anyway."

The houses provided the perfect conditions for growing the mold the mask wearers demanded so now every house standing was controlled by the overfarmers. What the nglaeylyaethm used the mold for, I had no idea. The question of why they did anything they did was always secondary to the hard truth that they would always see that their demands were met no matter how strange or inhuman they might be. Their power over us meant they didn't have to give reasons.

"I hate those houses," Uli said, looking at them.

"So do I."

When we got to the cabin I saw it had fallen apart even more than I remembered. Aside from the still-standing fireplace and chimney, the place was completely flattened. I spotted the piece of mask wearer flesh I'd remembered, really just a chunk from part of a tentacle, among the debris. I used a branch to reach through what might once have been a door or window frame and fished it out. The tentacle chunk would provide about enough material to make a small hat. It was pathetic but I supposed by making the effort to salvage that sad scrap I would be demonstrating to Uli just how desperate we were, and it would at least provide Kolb something he could use to practice fashioning the flesh into something useful.

When Uli and I returned we found Shully sobbing on the floor. Pixa was beside her wearing a surprisingly adult expression of concern as her little hands held her mother's hand. The fire was out, but the entire space inside the tent stank of something like burnt hair and overcooked insects.

Kolb was gone.

I asked Uli to look after Pixa while I took Shully aside. Shully took a few sharp breaths, calmed down enough to talk, then led me outside to explain what had happened.

Apparently it had taken Shully most of the morning to get Kolb to sit still long enough for her to start teaching him how to stitch the husks. He seemed to get the hang of it after sewing a few stitches into a small piece she'd cut for him to practice with. Shully thought he was ready to work on the big sheet that would make up most of the next tent, so she'd set him up to work on that. Then she had to leave to take Pixa to the toilet pit.

When they came back, the tent was filled with smoke. Kolb had thrown the big piece of husk he was supposed to be stitching into the fire. Flames licked up around its cracked, blackened surface. Kolb was running in circles around it, waving his hands, crying furiously and screaming at nothing. Shully pulled the ruined husk out from the fire and dragged it outside to stomp out the flames.

Back inside, Kolb was still screaming. "I tried to calm him down," she said. "I tried to get him to let me hold him, tried to give him something to eat, something to drink. Nothing worked." Then Pixa started crying. She suppressed her anger about the ruined husk and as gently as she could repeated, "Hush, hush." He was screaming the whole time.

Then Kolb lunged at her and she shoved him back, hard enough that he fell and hit his face against the ground. "I shouldn't have pushed him so hard," she said. "But you should have seen his eyes. I didn't know what he would do.

I just reacted."

Blood was pouring out of Kolb's nose when he stood back up. Shully tried to calm herself down, tried to show she was sorry for hitting him while also remaining firm in her intention to teach the boy that wasting a mask wearer husk was a wrong not soon forgiven. She tried telling him that the tent they could have made from the material he'd destroyed could have been sold for enough tokens to feed the family for at least a week.

Kolb didn't understand. He stomped. He spit on the floor. He screamed again. Pixa kept crying. Shully's attention shifted to the girl. That's when Kolb ran. She tried to chase him, but she'd picked up Pixa and the boy was fast. He ducked into the small crowd surrounding the communal wash tub. By the time Shully reached the crowd, he was gone, and none of the bathers gathered there could say where he went.

She blamed herself. She'd collapsed in tears when she returned, and that was when Uli and I walked in.

"You let him run away?" shouted Uli as she stepped outside, fists clenched. She'd been listening.

"Where's Pixa?" I asked her.

"I'm going after him," she said. "I'm going to find

him."

Shully stepped around Uli and into the tent. "Pixa's fine," she called from inside.

"You're not going anywhere," I told Uli. But she knew I wouldn't stop her from trying to find her brother. She gave me a look that said as much, then turned and ran. "Wait!" I called after her. "Let me come with you!" But she was gone.

"Let her go," said Shully as I joined her and Pixa in the tent. "She doesn't need your help."

For the next several hours I worried neither would return, but Shully was right. Well after dark, Uli returned with Kolb. In the meantime Shully and I had agreed not to punish Kolb any further for what had happened that day, nor would we punish Uli for her disobedience. We decided we'd just start over tomorrow as if this awful day hadn't happened.

But when Uli and Kolb returned, they were carrying armloads of stolen beets and dried fish. They gasped for breath, they'd been running, and spoke over one another in panicky voices. It was obvious they were being pursued.

Soon we heard the dogs outside. After a few minutes, our tent was surrounded.

A large hand pushed open the flap of our tent. Molc Fisher, a wide, imposing man with thick gray eyebrows and a missing ear, shoved his way inside. He was the leader of the Fisher clan, the rulers of the river bank who controlled all nearby encampments' supply of fish.

In his hand I glimpsed the flash of a fish knife.

"Shully and Thorner Tenter," he said. "I hope your family is weathering the storm."

"My hope for your family is the same," Shully replied, the traditional response to Molc's traditional declaration of a quarrel to be resolved between our families.

"B'jin, Lavo," called Molc to people outside. "In the tent here. Now!"

Molc's small, muscular twin sons entered our tent. Each held the leash of one of the hairless, red-eyed dogs the Fishers are known to breed to protect their food stores from thieves and rogue bears. The animals wore mask wearer husk harnesses with sacks hanging down the sides so the dogs could be used as pack animals. Shully had made the harnesses for the Fishers.

"Now show me your food stores," said Molc.

"Mr. Fisher," I pleaded. "This won't happen again. The children—"

"The children are your responsibility," said Molc. "You know the law. A caught thief must offer all to those from whom he thieved."

"Please," said Shully.

"Show me your food stores," Molc repeated.

10

MAYBE WITH MORE TIME the children could have been taught the tenting trade.

Maybe if Molc hadn't taken our food, starvation would not have seemed like an immediate threat.

Maybe if any number of circumstances had been different, we would not have been so desperate.

But things were as they were, so Shully and I made a decision: I would find work at the mold farm. I would work on the farm only for as long as necessary for me to earn the tokens we needed. Once we replenished our food stores and rebuilt our tenting business, I would quit.

The farm workers' encampment was a half-day's journey away.

I arrived before sunrise and in the fog found the three dozen or so people there just starting to stir from their sleeping bags and tents. They set about their early morning activities silently, almost mechanically.

Five of the farm workers, all wrapped in blankets and rags, had gathered in a circle around the glowing embers of a dying fire. They were warming their breakfast, some kind of porridge. Their ghostly silence made me nervous. I joined their circle. They neither looked at me nor welcomed me. But I was handed a bowl of porridge. I accepted it gratefully.

Soon I was following the workers to the place where they mustered each day hoping to be chosen for work. The location was marked by a bend in the dirt road where a half-buried hunk of wreckage, some kind of wartime aircraft, jutted out from the ground, its wings askew like a crushed insect.

We all lined up in a row facing the road. Occasionally I overheard hushed talk among the others. No one spoke to me. Why should they? I was a new competitor. If I was chosen, one of the others would not be.

I tried not to draw attention to myself. I was ready to fight if anyone tried to force me away. Not that fighting would do any good. There were so many of them and only one of me. Better to earn their begrudging acceptance of my presence than to force my way in to the group.

The sun rose. We stood waiting like that for hours. I felt a familiar urge that I needed to relieve, and tried using it to connect with the man standing beside me: I asked him where one goes when one has to pee. He turned his head and stared at me. His hair was gray and his face was tanned and tired. A big smile stretched across his face, and then he laughed as if what I'd said was the funniest thing he'd ever heard. Instead of answering me, he turned and whispered to others beside him, who also laughed and then openly leaned forward to get a better look at me. No one answered my question. In the end I stepped out of line, ducked behind a tree, then returned to my place in line after I finished. Those around me were still chuckling to themselves, apparently at my expense. I didn't yet understand why.

Eventually a big mechanoid pulling a large metal cart came marching up the dirt road and stopped in front of us.

The mechanoid was three times taller than the tallest among us. Those it selected it picked up in its claw-like hands under their armpits, as if they were children, swiveled its waist around, and placed them one by one into the cart. The cart looked like it was large enough to fit all of us and still have extra room left over. The mechanoid stepped in front of me, stopped, and my wish to be chosen was diminished by my fear of that machine. What was it looking for when it looked me over with its single glass eye? I didn't know. When it moved on, I felt both relieved and disappointed. By the time it was finished and started marching back to the mold farm, it had chosen about half of the waiting workers.

The remaining farm workers relaxed. Some withdrew to their tents. Some huddled together under a dead tree to lean their heads back, pull down an eyelid, and dose themselves with shard. The two who were left out of the five who had been sitting by the fire returned to the same place.

I approached the fire and offered to gather more wood. The workers ignored me. I gathered the wood anyway, and when I was done tossed in a handful of dry sticks that quickly ignited. I was positioning a log on top of the burning sticks when someone tapped my shoulder.

Standing behind me was a squat, stubbly man. He introduced himself as Gar, then reached around me to put a kettle on the fire. I told him my name and that I'd come hoping to work on the farm. When the kettle whistled, he pulled it out with a stick. Then, using a leaf to protect his hand from being burned on the metal handle, he poured hot water into ceramic cups with handfuls of herbs inside. He handed me a cup and handed the other to the other person by the fire, Luolo, a small, older woman. She was sharpening a knife. Luolo gave Gar a look of disapproval. Gar shrugged.

"The machine isn't going to choose you," Gar said. "If you want to learn how to be chosen, you're going to have to wait."

I was annoyed. Of course things would have to be more complicated than they seemed. I became instantly infuriated. I didn't have a clue yet why or how the system for joining the mold farm's workforce was unfair but I knew immediately that it would be unfair. I closed my eyes and clenched and unclenched my jaw and inhaled and exhaled. In a minute I was calm enough to ask, "How long will I have to wait?"

Gar and Luolo drank their tea. I knew neither would offer an answer.

"If you know how to be chosen, why are you still here? Why didn't the mechanoid put you two on its cart?"

They didn't answer.

Neither of them, nor anyone else, said anything more to me for the rest of the day.

Exhausted and annoyed, I eventually put up the small tent I'd brought and went to sleep.

It was dark when I awoke. The fire was tall and crackling now and lots of people were standing around it. The chosen workers had returned. Gar was ladling them stew from a metal pot. It smelled like onions.

I stepped in line behind the others, hoping Gar would let me have some. The others stood in my way. They made a wall of their backs and chatted casually with each other while keeping me away.

They were purposely blocking me from reaching the stew and acting as if they didn't see me.

I thought they would leave after finishing their stew but there was always someone standing in my way, even after everyone seemed to have finished eating. I was about to go back to my tent hungry when I heard Gar say my name. "Thorner, take the pot and clean it."

Now the others let me through. I took the pot, its handles still warm from the fire, and carried it to the swampy ditch at the edge of the encampment. I put my hand in the pot and felt a few soft chunks of stewed roots had been left among the stems and bones at the bottom. Everything in the pot that seemed edible, I ate. Then I crouched down and with my fingers started scooping mud out of the ditch. I dug until I'd made a hole in the mud containing enough muddy water to rinse out the pot. I filled it halfway and returned it to the fire to boil away any clinging stew bits.

After dumping out the water and giving it a final scrape, I returned to my tent. Luolo was inside. "I sleep here now," she said. I tried pulling her out. She put her knife against my neck. I relented. Anyway, I had already slept.

I pulled back an eyelid and rationed myself a half-dose of shard and laid my back against a tree.

I felt a familiar tingling sensation behind my eyes.

The tingling expanded and grew into what always seemed like a feeling too large for my head to contain, then receded into a numbing warmth pulsing back and forth between the front of my head and the back of my head.

Then the waves of tingles descended from my head down through my body and toward my toes.

In my field of vision vague shapes started dancing

in the dark.

Finally, a temporary state of semiconscious catatonic bliss cocooned my mind, accelerating time until after sunrise. The drug's aftereffects left me feeling brittle and raw.

In that murky state I watched the fire flicker until it was time to will myself upright and stand along the road with the others again.

11

EVERY DAY, THE MOLD FARM WORKERS lined up to be chosen. Every day, I joined them. Every day, the mechanoid passed me by.

On the morning of the sixth day I was told why I'd never be chosen. At least, not as I was.

I was sitting at the fire pit, toasting some kind of big white grub on the end of a stick. Gar sat down next to me. He had been chosen every day after that first day. He looked tired. "You don't have the mark," he said.

"What mark?"

"This mark," he said, pointing to the side of his neck. There was a design there, a complex looking network of lines radiating outward from a tangled mass in the center. I had noticed this mark on him and some of the others but had assumed its significance had something to do with its wearers' religion or tribal affiliation. "Everyone who wants to work on the mold farm has to wear the mark. If you don't have the mark, the mechanoids won't choose you. The others didn't want me to tell you. Each time someone new starts, it means less work for those of us who already have the mark. Less work, fewer tokens, smaller rations. We all have so little, we're not very good at sharing what we have with newcomers."

I was furious.

Day after day I had dutifully lined up along the road with the others, naively hoping to be selected. The others knew the mechanoid would pass me by every time. They were waiting for me to give up.

I wished I could give up.

But I had already spent so much time trying to work on the farm. Giving up now would have meant the days I'd spent trying to start had been completely wasted.

I didn't have any more time to waste.

My family was depending on me.

"Where do I get the mark?"

"You don't want the mark," said Gar. His face was serious. "You should go."

"Tell me."

Gar sighed. "You have to go to Hecla. Find the riverbed bordering the farm and follow it for maybe half a day. You'll find her at the bottom of the valley."

12

I FOLLOWED GAR'S DIRECTIONS. The walk was slow going. Chest-high weeds covered the dried-up riverbed except where there was cracked mud or stagnant puddles. On either side of the riverbed, pines grew thick enough to block the sky. The low point of the valley was so dark and cool it was like the inside of a cave. There the dusty ruins of a half-sunken barge stood in the middle of a pile of shipping containers that must have fallen off of it long ago.

Fifteen or so small, childlike shapes crept out of the containers as I approached. They were clothed entirely in muddy rags and hoods concealed their faces. The things crawled on their hands and knees as if they were pretending to be animals. Seeing them was somehow like seeing live insects scuttling about in one's food stores. I was immediately repulsed.

On the half-sunken barge, three shipping containers remained stacked one on top of the other. A gaunt, shrouded figure emerged from between the curtains covering the opening of the uppermost container. The figure pulled itself out and on top of the desultory structure and stood there looking down at me. "This way, stranger," said the figure in a deep and feminine voice. I knew right away that this was Hecla.

The childlike shapes kept their distance as I walked past. Ankle-deep mud made moving quickly impossible. I was sure I would need a running start if I wanted to attempt hoisting myself over the side of the barge. Thankfully, when I reached the barge a shadowy shape peered over the edge, then tossed me down a rope ladder. I climbed to the top and stepped onto the barge and found a second rope ladder hanging down from the curtained entrance to the top container.

I climbed up and crawled through the curtain.

The container was rank inside with smoke, sweat, and an unearthly funk I couldn't name. Hecla crouched beside a small fire at the far end of the container. In the firelight I saw one wall was lined with shelves filled with strange tools and devices. I recognized some of it as medical equipment salvaged from a bygone era. The sharp things the midwife had when Shully gave birth to Pixa came to mind. The memory gave me a shiver. On the opposite wall were glass aquariums of various sizes, some empty, some filled with a strange, opaque liquid.

Hecla stood and flipped a switch. Painfully bright light filled the space, and I flinched. She pulled back her hood and locked an eye on me. The other eye was missing. The way the scarred skin had sunken in around where it should have been, I guessed a fair portion of the orbital bones that used to frame it were missing too.

I was amazed. I tried not to show it. The significance of her scar was immediately obvious to me: she was an ex-para-sight. She had been part of the mask wearers' surveillance apparatus. Yet somehow she had removed herself from their control. I couldn't imagine how this was possible. But there she was, standing in front of me: living proof that even para-sights can escape a life of service to their tentacled masters.

"You're here for the mark," she said. I said yes, I was. She unfolded a chair. "Sit down." I did as I was told. She unfolded another chair and placed a small table in front of me. In one hand she held a small device with a tiny beam of red light shining out of it. In the other she held a marker. She aimed the beam of light at my neck. "Don't move," she said. After the device clicked, she leaned forward and drew an X on the skin just above my right clavicle. I could smell her stale breath. The moment felt uncomfortably intimate.

I made a comment in reference to her being an ex-para-sight. I said I thought it was reassuring to see an example of someone who had freed themself from a life of noodle service.

"I'm still a noodle server," she said humorlessly. "It's just no longer my body that I sell. Now I sell yours."

She got up to retrieve what looked like a black pyramid from the wall of aquariums. She carried it with both hands in a way I could tell it was heavy and probably dangerous. When she placed it on the table in front of me it rattled as if it were full of nuts or sea shells. Silently she unscrewed the top of the pyramid, then reached into it with a small pair of metal tongs. The tongs came out holding what looked like an acorn-sized black teardrop.

"Now lay your head back," she said. She placed a hand under my chin and pushed my head back. "This is going to hurt. And it's not the worst part."

"Wait," I said. "What are you doing?"

Hecla sighed. "Giving you the mark. Here," she grabbed a scum-dappled mirror off the wall and placed it on the table in front of me. "Go ahead and watch if you want."

I took the mirror. It was awkward trying to aim it at the place on my neck that she'd marked with my head leaning back. She put a coarse hand on my chest and hissed at me to hold still and for just a second, I obeyed. Then she jammed the pointy end of the teardrop into the X on my neck and I felt the spot become suddenly and alarmingly very alive.

Hecla backed away quickly.

In the mirror I saw the teardrop had hatched into a writhing mass of what looked like black hair that fast burrowed under my skin. From the black clot under where the X had been the wormlike things spread in all directions, toward my chest, my shoulder, my head, their bodies making lines under my skin as they advanced.

"They want to bore into your bones and make nests in your marrow," Hecla said calmly as she rummaged among the mechanical things on her wall of tool shelves. "Ah," she said as she turned and brought me a piece of paper and an ink pen. "Here's your contract. Sign here," she pointed to an X on the bottom of the page much like the X she'd drawn on my neck. "You don't have time to read the whole thing. But you should know it means you owe me a certain sum for my service, a sum I can't imagine you'll be able to pay off in less than five years. Agree to the terms, I stop the worms."

"What?" As the things burrowed, the feeling of them advancing under my skin was something like a sharp tickle. I felt them beginning to reach around the back of my neck, into my armpit, behind my ear.

Gently, Hecla nudged the contract closer. "Sign."

I took the pen and scribbled an approximation of my name.

Hecla then picked up an ancient-looking piece of machinery. She held it up to her face and seemed to look through it with her good eye, then pressed a button on it. A blinding flash of light burst out of the machine. Colored spots oozed across my field of vision. I tried blinking them away.

I checked the mirror. The worms had stopped. The loose ends of some that had not fully entered my neck lay dead against my skin. Hecla took the contract and wiped the dissolving creatures away with a rag.

"Now get some rest," she said, helping me up. She guided me toward a large, soft reclining chair in the corner of her container. I sat and held up the mirror. The darkening stain on my neck was exactly like the mark the others wore.

Five years, I thought.

This was not the plan Shully and I had agreed on.

I tried not to think about it. I had completely lost control of the situation. Worrying would not make anything any better. All I had to do was what I was supposed to do, and everything would work out. Maybe not exactly the way Shully and I had planned. But for the best, even if we met unexpected challenges along the way.

The important thing was that the children could rely on us to provide for them.

Hecla made tea and served me a tiny cup. It tasted like dead grass.

I took two sips and fell asleep.

I WOKE UP TO HECLA CURSING and splashing as she felt around in the aquariums stacked against the wall. I don't think I was out for long. I couldn't believe I'd let down my guard so much I'd fallen asleep. "What's happening?" I said.

Hecla cursed again. She was pouring the fluid out from one aquarium into another. Then she repeated this with another aquarium, and then another. If the pouring resulted in one of the containers becoming too full, she would violently poke around in the opaque fluid with a large slotted spoon.

"What's happening?" I said again.

"What's happening is, I'm going to have to trust you not to ruin me," she said, still sloshing the liquid around with her spoon. "I don't trust anyone. And I have no reason to think I should trust you. In fact I think you definitely should not be trusted. But I don't have a choice." She pulled the dripping spoon from the ooze and regarded it balefully. "Unless I decide to kill you now. I'm sure I could kill you. But I don't want to kill you." She dropped the spoon, then turned to rummage through the equipment on the opposite wall. "Not that you're special or anything. It's just that I've killed enough already. It's not you in particular I don't want to kill. I just don't want to kill. So I don't think I'm going to kill you. But I do think not killing you is going to be another mistake. So now I have to accept that on top of one huge mistake I've made today, I'm going to make another."

"Kill me?" I said, sitting up on the cot and immediately very awake and aware of how easy it would have been for Hecla to do just that while I slept.

"No, I've already decided. I'm going to trust you. And because of it, it's *you* who is going to kill *me*."

"It's alright," I said. "You can trust me."

"No, I can't," she replied. "You're desperate. If you weren't desperate, you wouldn't be here, receiving the mark, ready to line up for work on the mold farm. If I know anything, I know the desperate can't be trusted."

I wanted to run away. But I was curious about what Hecla was saying. I didn't quite understand. Maybe if she kept talking I'd understand. "Why is it so important for you to trust me?"

Hecla sighed. "Because I'm all out of hygienic voids. I must have used the last one and not realized, or it might have crawled away, or something, I don't know." She gestured toward a large tank full of the strange liquid. "If you go to work on that farm and Weckett finds out I gave you the mark without implanting a void in you first, he'll destroy me. But I know you're going to go to work on that farm. So I know Weckett is going to find out. So that's all there is to it."

"I promise I won't let Weckett find out."

Hecla laughed. "Thanks," she said. "You seem sincere. But you need to understand, when you're caught, it's not going to end well for you either. And if you think snitching on me might increase your chances of survival, know this: I will be the end of you."

I told her I understood.

The grim look on Hecla's one-eyed face haunted me as I climbed down the stack of containers.

In the mud, four of the crawling hooded figures

surrounded me. The rank smell of their bodies was so strong I couldn't help recoiling even in the open air. They seemed weak and clumsy. I surmised I could easily push past them, but I didn't want to touch them.

Hecla watched me from her perch. "If you're carrying any shard on you, they can smell it," she shouted down. "You should give them some. They need it more than you."

All I had left were two capsules. To be giving them anything worth giving, I would have to give all of it to them, a half capsule each. "Why would they think I'm carrying shard?" I called back up to her. "And even if I had any, why should I give it away?"

"They're end-stage addicts," Hecla shouted back. "I said they can smell it on you. Without it, they'll die. With it, you'll eventually become them."

A bony hand emerged from one of the figure's ragged sleeves to claw weakly at my coat. Its hood partly fell away to reveal the collapsed face of what was once a man. He moaned. His deranged expression and ruined mouth made me doubt he was capable of speech. Then the other figures started trying to clamber around and over this moaning man to try to get to me.

They moved stiffly, as if their bodies were brittle in a way that meant they'd probably injure themselves trying to reach me. And if they injured themselves reaching for me, Hecla probably would hold me responsible. I didn't want that. Possibly I would find myself working for her instead of for my family, who I reminded myself were the only reason any of this pathetic struggle had any semblance of purpose at all.

I leapt away from the addicts and jogged a few paces out of their reach. I found the egg-like capsules in my pocket and held them in my hand.

Slowly, the addicts crawled after me.

Backing away, I imagined carefully emptying the powdered contents of the capsules into their sunken eyes.

I imagined throwing the unsplit capsules over their heads so they would stop crawling after me and go fight among themselves for the doses instead.

I imagined kicking them away until they were too injured to follow me.

And then I turned and ran, doses still clenched in my hand, feeling as desperate as Hecla had accused me of being.

14

I SUCCEEDED IN PUTTING a safe distance between myself and Hecla's shard addicts and followed the dried-up riverbed back toward the farm workers' encampment. I vowed never to let myself become what those addicts were.

I couldn't stop thinking about the man's face and the man's moan.

To put him out of my mind while I walked I focused on the instructions Hecla gave me for avoiding being caught without a hygienic void.

"One. Don't talk about it," she said. "You make up a story about what it was like to have a void put inside you or what it feels like, the other farm workers will know right away that you're lying. The others have actually been through it. Never forget that.

"Two," she continued. "No toilet breaks. The entire

reason the nglaeylyaethm want farm workers to have a void inside of them is so their bodies no longer produce waste. They're afraid you'll contaminate the farm. So: no piss, no shit. Not at the encampment where anyone can see you, and certainly not on the farm.

"Three. Don't get caught. You get caught, it's the end of you, and it's the end of me. Which, again, also means the end of you."

Of course I was scared of being caught, though not as scared as I should have been. Mostly I felt relieved about not having a hygienic void put inside of me. I was hopeful, now that I had the mark, that I would have a fair chance of being selected for a day of work on the farm.

It was dark when Luolo met me at the edge of the encampment. She had a look on her face like she was going to pull her knife on me. Instead, she handed me a plastic tube, the kind I knew Shully would have used to send a message. "This came for you," she said.

The seal on the tube had been broken, but the message inside was intact. I read it immediately.

Everyone was doing fine without me, Shully wrote, but she missed me intensely and wanted me back home as soon as possible. Pixa missed me too. She'd gotten into the habit of talking about me so much it had ceased to be annoying and become a joke between Shully and Uli. Apparently Pixa always wanted her bedtime stories to be about me. According to her this was so she would dream about me. Meanwhile, Uli's tenting lessons were progressing. As for Kolb, Stoker the elder had taken him under his wing and was teaching the boy about gathering wood to feed the communal fire.

Stoker and others had taken pity on them, she wrote, and were sharing what food and water they could spare in exchange for tent repairs. Shully felt grateful for their neighbors' generosity, but she knew it wouldn't last if she had to depend on them much longer.

The message from home was a relief.

Everything was going according to plan.

What remained was for me to hold up my end of the bargain.

I followed Luolo back to the fire, where she handed me the dirty pot. The others had already eaten. I made a meal of what I could scrape off the bottom, then cleaned it like I knew I was expected to.

15

THE NEXT DAY I LINED UP with the other farm workers and when the mechanoid came, it picked me up and put me in its cart.

Just like that, having the mark made all the difference.

And I was chosen the next day, and the next day, and the day after that too.

For the first few weeks, I was chosen three or four days a week.

Each day after I was chosen, the huge morning mechanoid would deliver me to one of the garages where the smaller, eight-foot-tall mold farming mechanoids were kept. These smaller mechanoids did most of the work in the part of the farm I was assigned to.

My first task was to activate these eight-foot mechanoids. I checked their oil and fuel levels and cranked a couple cranks and switched a couple switches and they would shudder to life, inner fans and gears spinning. After warming up for a minute or two, they would step out of their charging stations and arrange themselves in a single-file line. Then they'd march to wherever we were supposed to be doing our farm work for the day. I fell in line behind them. For the rest of the day, I followed their lead.

　　　The other workers from the encampment perform-ed the same tasks on other parts of the farm. Every once in a while other human underfarmers would join me. Even when working with others I knew, like Gar and Luolo, who had returned my tent after I returned from getting the mark, we hardly acknowledged one another. We didn't speak. We hardly made eye contact. "Being a talker is a sure way to make the morning mechanoid stop selecting you," Gar told me one night back at the encampment. So when we worked, we took our cues from the mechanoids. On the job, we just acted like flesh-and-blood machines.

　　　We followed the mechanoids down roads between rows of old houses whose faded colors and sagging facades gave them the look of completely defeated things. When we reached the building that would be our work site for the day, we split into teams of two or three with most of the teams being made up entirely of mechanoids. Each team entered a different house.

The houses were huge. All of them had a ground floor with enough space to shelter three or four families. The basement levels were just as big. Most had a second floor with even more living space, and, above that, an attic. Furniture, the kinds I knew about from stories, inhabited the rooms. Couches, tables, beds, bathtubs, refrigerators, and so on, all rotten and covered in hairy layers of yellow, pink, and gray mold.

The work was simple. First the mechanoids would scrape away thick sheets of mold into special containers. Then they stacked the containers onto a wheeled cart. I followed behind, pushing an angled blade into the corners and crevices the mechs could not reach, collecting as much of the remaining mold as possible in separate smaller containers I carried with me. I was told it was very important never to mix mold harvested by humans with the mechanoid-harvested mold.

The owner of the mold farm was Overfarmer Weckett. He was a large man and he always wore sunglasses and white coveralls. It was unbelievable how white his white coveralls were.

A few times a week he'd drive around the farm in a small motorized vehicle. During my early days on the farm, he'd occasionally park his vehicle outside the house where I was working and beckon me outside to walk with him. He seemed interested in hearing me talk about my family and my experience selling tents. He asked about my gray hands. I assured him it was because I worked with shedded mask wearer skins. He said if I kept working hard I might someday be able to move up from scraping mold. "One day, you could be selling the mold," he said as if it was obvious such a move should be extremely desirable to me.

After Weckett finished asking me questions, he would share his opinions about the state of the world with me. I could tell he liked having an audience, and I was a good listener. I found I had a knack for nodding along to his monologues and reacting in a way he appreciated, even when I wasn't interested or didn't understand what he was trying to say. In these moments it was clear he would be talking for a while and it was my job to listen and understand and agree with what he said. He was charming in his way and I have to say at the time a lot of what he said made sense, though there were many times when I found myself making myself appear to agree with him even when I did not.

"People who are too proud to serve our friends, the nglaeylyaethm, are fools," he said. "The truth is, it was our war with them that killed the world. No one remembers exactly why we went to war, or considers that things might have been better for humanity had we not put up a fight. I wonder if those people who chose to fight ever stopped to think what it would be like for humans after they lost. I don't think they did. Anyway the important thing is, *they* won. We lost. Anyone who wants to climb up from the muck and make a reasonably comfortable life for themselves has to accept that the nglaeylyaethm *own* humanity."

We walked the dirty path between houses and swatted at clouds of insects hovering in the air in front of us.

"Of course, they're just like us," Weckett went on. "They want stuff. Different stuff from what we want, but stuff nonetheless. They want what they want, and if you can find a way to give it to them, they'll reward you and they'll come back for more. The only thing is, you want to get them their stuff, you've got to be willing to work. That's why I like you. I can tell you're willing to work. Work is the most important thing. Hard work is the foundation of this farm and I'm proud of that."

We stopped in front of a house that was much larger than the others. It had towers and turrets and a wraparound porch, all completely covered in a thick layer of multicolored mold.

"Do you know how they use the mold?" he asked me.

I shook my head. He smirked. Of course he'd assumed I didn't know, and he'd been correct. I kept smiling, but there was something about the joy he took from being correct about my ignorance that made me want to tear his face off. The moment passed.

He turned toward me. "They use the mold to make these crystal chambers. Marvelous things. That's how they replenish themselves. I think the chambers are how they evolved past eating and sleeping, how they survive traveling across the vastness of space."

He bent close to speak softly into my ear. "And in exchange for running this farm for them, they've given me a crystal chamber of my own. It's amazing. I haven't had anything to eat in eight years and I don't miss it. I just step into the chamber, and close the lid, and it feels like the most exquisite bliss. It's like becoming a human hard-on, like dissolving into drunkenness and sex and dreams and at the same time more physically fulfilling than eating a big piece of meat." He straightened himself up and continued in a louder voice, "Of course, the crystals in my chamber are in constant need of replenishment. That's where our mold farm comes in."

I admitted I could see the appeal of having a place to seal myself off from the world, to forget about everything and never worry about going hungry. I kept to myself that this basically was why I liked shard so much.

"Keep working hard," said Weckett, as if any amount of underfarming work I could do could lead to my having a crystal chamber of my own.

Walking back to the house where I would go back to scraping mold for the rest of the day, I asked why I have to keep the mold I collect separate from the mold the mechanoids collect.

Weckett chuckled. "Because the mold the mechanoids collect is for the nglaeylyaethm, and the mold you and the other human underfarmers collect is for me." He added, "It's the noodles that insist all humans who work on the farm be implanted with a hygienic void. They're strict about this, even if you never come into direct contact with the mold they're going to use. Otherwise, they'd refuse to buy my mold, and I'd be out of business. Believe it or not, they even made me swallow one of those fucked up things. So there are ways we're all the same here on the farm."

Only once did I ever see Weckett actually go inside of one of the houses. I was working on the floor, under what once had been someone's dining room table, scraping away mold that came off of its underside like hanks of damp hair. The mechanoids were working upstairs. When they moved around, stomping their big metal feet as they walked, clouds of spores came loose from the ceiling.

Weckett came in through the front door. I didn't recognize him at first. A white mask that made a hissing sound when he breathed covered his face. He held the door open, and a mask wearer came in after him, followed by a woman with short gray hair, the thing's pet. The creature moved cautiously, most of its mass of tentacles drawn in tightly. As Weckett beckoned them inside, the woman, who wore clothes the same rusty color as the creature's skin, faced him and so did the mask wearer's mask-wearing tentacle.

I couldn't quite hear what Weckett was saying to them. I assumed he was explaining the mold farming process. He stooped down and used a metal tool to scrape a chunk of mold out from a corner of the foyer where they stood. He held out the mold in a gloved hand. Using the tool, he poked it apart. The woman and the tentacle leaned forward to examine the contents of Weckett's hand.

It seemed like Weckett was about to lead the nglaeylyaethm and its pet up the stairs when the mask-wearing tentacle turned toward me.

I became very aware of the sounds my stomach was making. I hadn't eaten since early the previous day. I was hungry. Also I think my fear of being in the presence of the creature was having an effect on my digestive system. Either way, my gut was making noises I was sure it wouldn't be making if I'd had a hygienic void inside of me.

I was sure I was exposed.

The mask wearer's tentacles surrounded me. They moved the mold-covered chairs out from around the mold-covered table I was working under. They reached under the table all around me, sensing I don't know what about me. The thing's thick, mask-wearing tentacle ducked under too. It turned its mask toward me. It was as if it was looking directly at me. The mask it wore was a horrid parody of a human face: two black circles, apparent approximation of eyes, were on one side of the face. A withered nose-like structure protruded from the other. A slanted, too-wide mouth was carved underneath. And there also, crouching on the floor and peering out from behind the tentacles, was the pet. Her dead, indifferent eyes stared.

My stomach gurgled. I felt hot.

I looked at the mask wearer and I looked at its companion. Could they sense my uninterrupted digestive tract? Could they tell it was inhabited by nothing but my own waste? I wondered, was the companion a complete puppet for the thing, or could she still think her own thoughts? Would her thoughts recognize the unfairness of her complete subservience compared to my relative freedom? Could she sense and resent my hygienic void avoidance? Or, if she could sense my disobedience without passing that knowledge along to her master, would she approve?

The mask wearer probed my face with its thin tentacles. The tentacles felt like they were somehow both spongy and strong. Then the mask-wearing tentacle pressed in close to my face. Its forehead pushed against my forehead. I was too afraid to breathe.

I asked myself: If it could sense my lack of a hygienic void, it wouldn't be touching me, would it? And if its curiosity about me wasn't about my secret, what was it about? Was it disgusted? Afraid? Did it think I was cute, like a rat kept as a pet? Did it pity me, or hate me? Or was its interest purely scientific, cold and detached?

There was no way to tell. However it felt about me, there was nothing I could do about it, no matter what it felt, if it felt anything at all.

To it, I was nothing.

Before it, my powerlessness was absolute.

And then, after several seconds, the mask wearer withdrew.

I allowed myself to breathe. I kept completely still as it followed Weckett up the stairs. The companion seemed to hesitate at the bottom of the stairs. The stairway wasn't very wide; she may just have been waiting to follow behind the thing. For an instant I thought maybe she wanted to say something to me. Maybe she was powerless to do so. Maybe she just didn't know what to say.

It was hard for me to stop thinking about the mask wearer and its pet suddenly being interested in me and then just as suddenly forgetting about me.

Perhaps it intended to express its suspicions about me to Weckett in private, I thought.

I realized I was projecting human thoughts and intentions onto the nglaeylyaethm that I had no reason to think were there. To it, I was not a person but a thing, an organism-tool that either did what it was supposed to do or did not. It was silly to think of it caring enough about my feelings to bother going through the trouble of gossiping behind my back.

Still under the table, I went back to scraping mold. I could hear Weckett's voice from upstairs. He did love having an audience. And for the first time I also heard what must have been the woman's voice. I strained to hear what she was saying. I couldn't make out a thing.

Not wanting to draw further attention to myself, I stayed under the table, collecting as much mold as I could, until Weckett, the mask wearer, and the woman descended the stairs. Only silence passed between them now and they said nothing more as they exited the house.

The next day when the morning mechanoid did not choose me I was sure my secret had been discovered and that I'd never work on the farm again.

Hecla would come for me.

She'd have me killed.

Would Shully and Pixa and Uli and Kolb survive?

I reassured myself they would. But would they be forced into serving the nglaeylyaethm?

Could my failure mean they will have to work for the likes of Jolm? Or sell themselves as para-sights? Or as pets?

I thought about that happening to Pixa. Her little head sticking out of one of Jolm's sacks. Her being prodded and kicked over by another pet inspecting her for the nglaeylyaethm. A rust-colored tentacle forcing itself into the back of her head.

She doesn't deserve any of this. She deserves better than me as her protector. As the person standing between her and becoming a slave to mask-wearing tentacle heaps. As her father.

She deserves better than this world she needs to be protected from.

I couldn't let that happen. I had to fight. I had to work. I had to do whatever I could do.

But I didn't know what to do.

And now, discovered and exposed and useless as I

knew I was, fury and hopelessness consumed me.

I was ready to unleash my rage against anyone or anything that would stop me from doing what I had to do. And what I had to do was protect Shully and Pixa and Uli and Kolb so they would have other ways to survive besides selling themselves to those things.

However I could, I would keep my body between them and that fate. Whatever had to do, I was prepared.

But then the next day, the morning mechanoid picked me up.

Still, for several days, I worried my secret was discovered.

But no. The morning mechanoid kept selecting me. And at the end of the week, I received my usual stack of tokens.

Gar and Nuolo could tell something was bothering me. I was sure of it. Gar gave me extra stew, which I didn't even eat and wound up putting back in the pot. When I returned from the nearby wooded area where I claimed to be foraging for food when I had to relieve myself, I noticed Nuolo slinking away from my tent. Inside, I found a half-dose of shard she must have left for me in the corner. I pulled down my eyelid and took it immediately.

The next time I saw Weckett, he mentioned he thought it was good for the nglaeylyaethm to see "clean, hard-working humans" like me on his mold farm. "Helps tamp down their prejudicial tendencies," he said.

16

AFTER A MONTH ON THE FARM I left for a day to take my tokens home.

I had eight in all—two for each week—after accounting for Hecla's cut, the encampment's cut, and the cut I set aside for shard.

When I arrived outside our tent, I hesitated.

After all I'd been through, I was afraid Shully would tell me it wasn't worth it. Now that I was indebted to Hecla, I didn't have a choice. I was going to have to work on the mold farm for years into the foreseeable future whether or not it was worth it. I wanted Shully to understand without me having to say anything to her that we needed to act like we were completely sure that me doing this job was worth it, even if we weren't really sure at all.

But if Shully had any doubt about whether my

mold farming work was worth everything it was putting me and my family through, she kept it to herself. What she was, was anxious.

I noticed her acting strangely after the initial round of hugs and kisses. There was something about the way she touched the mark Hecla put on my neck. I kept catching her stealing glances at it all evening long. She didn't ask any questions about where I had been or what it was like and for some reason this made me feel accused. It was as if she thought I had been replaced by a counterfeit version of myself.

We ate a big meal of stewed possum and roasted mushrooms. As we ate I asked her if there had been any problems while I was away and she said no, so I asked again and again. How could there not have been problems? I couldn't imagine an existence without problems. And, more to the point, I thought hearing stories about the family's everyday struggles would give me a sense of being connected to what was happening—and distract me from the difficulties of my underfarmer life. It felt like Shully was denying me this connection, this distraction. I didn't think it was fair. But I also knew I wasn't being fair to her either.

We wound up whispering sharp words across the table at each other until she had enough. She took me by the front of my shirt and pulled me outside, leaving Uli in charge inside, and told me she was tired and that she recognized I was tired. She demanded I stop twisting what was happening around me into a story of me being some kind of sad victim, at least while I was home.

I agreed I was tired and should try to do what she asked.

That night I played a game with Pixa that she'd made up. She called the game "wasp and worm." She pointed at me and said "wasp!" and then pointed at herself and said "worm!" Then I was supposed to make a buzzing noise and chase her, threatening, "I'm gonna sting you! I'm gonna sting you!" until I caught her and tickled her until she told me to stop.

Then we reversed roles. When it was her turn to be the wasp and my turn to be the worm, she would say "sting you, sting you" over and over again as menacingly as she could. Then she'd catch me and even though her attempts to tickle me with her little kid fingers didn't actually tickle, I never laughed harder in my life.

We played like that in the candlelight well past

when Pixa was supposed to go to sleep. Eventually Shully reminded us it was time to calm down. Pixa agreed to stop only after I promised I would still be home in the morning. She fell asleep in her bed almost immediately and when I joined Shully in ours, so did I.

Kolb woke up screaming in the middle of the night. Then Pixa woke up crying. I held her. "This is not unusual," Shully said as she got up to comfort Kolb. "There, there baby," I could hear her saying soothingly from the section of the tent where he and Uli slept. "Everything is alright."

He shrieked again.

Carrying Pixa in one arm, I got up to help. When I opened the flap that was the entrance to Uli and Kolb's section of the tent, I saw Shully reach for Kolb. He grabbed her arm and pulled it to his mouth and bit down until she bled. I rushed forward and smacked Kolb in the face, hard. He fell. When he sat up, he was sobbing uncontrollably. Blood trickled from his nose.

Uli came back. She must have gone outside to pee. I realized her absence must have been what had upset Kolb so much. She rushed to his side and put her arms around him. I saw him bite her too. As his teeth sunk in, she didn't even flinch.

17

ON THE ROAD BACK to the mold farmer encampment I noticed in the near distance one of the nglaeylyaethm's enormous crystal towers in the sky. I could see that things were dropping from the tower. Judging from where it hovered over ridge of wooded hills, I guessed that walking toward it would take me not much more than an hour or two out of my way. If there were husks among the rubbish, I could gather as much as I could carry and take them home to Shully. The delay would be well worth it.

I crossed fields and a hill covered with dead trees as I walked toward the crystal tower. Many of the trees had fallen, and climbing over them one by one made the trek over the hill more difficult than I thought it would be. The sun was high and hot and unforgiving on my skin. I was undoubtedly in the woods but the shadows of sticks offered almost no shade. I could feel my face and neck beginning to burn.

I'd lost sight of the crystal tower as I walked up the hill and saw it again only once I reached the top. There I saw it was floating directly above a lake. The lake was greenish black and the hollow remains of ancient vehicles lined its shores like a row of metal skulls.

A trail I found through the dead woods made going down the hill much easier than going up was.

When I came out of the woods at the bottom of the hill and looked up I could see what the crystal tower was dropping. I saw that the shapes falling out of the tower were not chunks of shedded mask wearer husks at all.

They were bodies, human bodies.

They fell limply from the tower every few minutes or so. For several minutes, I stood there watching them fall. Occasionally they landed with a splash. Most landed on what looked like a small island in the lake. I didn't want to get close enough to be sure, but I thought it looked like the island was made of bodies. It was hard to be sure because of the small trees and reeds growing out of it. If the island was made entirely of bodies there must be some that had been there for a long time.

I turned to cross back over the hill.

18

I LAY MY TOOLS side by side on the windowsill. Scraper. Curette. Pick.

A thick, rippled layer of gray-green growth carpeted the window. I lifted the curette, then set to work gouging mold out of the corner.

A crack of thunder shook the house. Soon, rain was pouring down outside against the windowpane. The polluted downpour filled the room with an unnatural metallic stink.

The old house creaked and groaned. I jumped when I heard a bang on the floor directly above me, and then a sound like something huge being ripped open, and then a sound like someone emptying sacks of broken glass onto the wooden floor.

And then the ceiling collapsed.

I tried to get out of the way.

I didn't move fast enough.

Rotten beams, bricks, and an entire refrigerator came down on me. Under the debris I felt a wet snap and gasped at the impossible pain.

My foot was broken. A moistness I knew was blood pooled warmly in my mangled boot.

Gray rain fell into the house through the ragged hole above me.

Almost immediately, the mechanoids that had been working in the house with me came to my side.

"Get help," I shouted. "My foot is broken! I can't move!"

The mechanoids just stood there. Their blank metal faces seemed to stare. I kept shouting, "Go! Go!" Finally, they left. I could feel my pulse throbbing in my foot. I was losing blood fast to the damp heap that pinned me.

The first time the mechanoids returned, they tried to move me. They grabbed my arms and pulled. The way I was positioned, it was like they were tearing my foot in two. They pulled until my screams sharpened to a shrill sound my ears scarcely recognized. Then they quit and left again.

The rain stopped.

I waited for what seemed like hours.

The wait forced me to face the limits of my will against my own body.

I had to pee. Oh god, I had to pee.

I closed my eyes. The pain in my foot kept coming back in waves that left me increasingly numb and increasingly awake. I think I might have lost consciousness right away were it not for the pressure building inside of me. Still, I willed the muscles tight until they began to twitch.

Trying to force my way out of the debris was useless. The pain in my abdomen was too much. The heap was too heavy. My foot, too broken.

I thought about how thirsty I had been when I first woke up that morning. So thirsty. And then there was Gar offering to let me drink from this bladder full of cider he had. I knew I'd gulped down more than I should. Now here I was. Would I ever forgive myself for allowing myself what had seemed at the time like such a small indulgence?

I blacked out.

When I dreamed, I dreamed of water coming out of me, gushing like my whole body from my chest down to my knees was a waterfall, and in the dream I was desperately and uselessly trying to force the water back into my body as it spilled continually between my fingers.

I awoke stinking of urine.

I saw that the mechanoids had returned. Mr. Weckett was with them.

In one arm he cradled a metal bowl.

MY JAW FEELS LOOSE. I spit and close my mouth, and it feels like my teeth don't meet the way they did before.

When I open my mouth, strings of yellowish fluid dribble from my lips.

One of the mechanoids is removing the debris from my body, piece by piece.

Weckett is gone now. Night has fallen.

A mechanoid puts its metal hands under my arms and starts to pull.

I feel my body coming free. My ruined foot rips apart.

I shriek through the unspeakable pain.

I CAN'T STOP SHIVERING. I don't know where I am.

I am wrapped in blankets. There is a fire somewhere nearby, I can smell it.

I am inside a tent that's large enough for other people to be standing inside of it with me. I think they're people, anyway. I guess they could be mechanoids. Or they could be something else.

Waves of tingly feelings are shooting up my leg from my foot, or what used to be my foot. However my leg ends now. If any part of my foot is still there, I really don't know.

The inside of the tent spins when I open my eyes. My field of vision tilts and blurs. I close my eyes again.

Suddenly, some kind of soup is in my mouth. Someone beside me is spooning it in. It's warm and thick.

Suddenly, I am covered in sweat and leaning over the side of the cot I've been lying on, vomiting.

Is that Gar beside me?

Is that Shully beside me?

Is that Hecla beside me?

Whoever they are, the shapes of them are all around me in the dark, talking about me as if I am not there.

"He's not eating."

"He sees things that aren't there. He doesn't see what's in front of him."

"Will he be able to walk?"

"He can't stay here like this forever."

"What are we going to do with him?"

21

FINGERS INTERTWINE WITH MY FINGERS. I open my eyes to a squint. It's Shully. Shully is here with me. The way she's framed by the light coming in through the mask wearer husk walls, I know it's a bright day outside.

"Hello," I say, the word emerging feebly from my lips. "You're here."

"I am," she says. She is smiling but her face is sad.

The room comes into focus. Kolb is beside Shully, and he's holding Pixa, who is asleep in his arms. Nuolo is there too. "You're all here," I say. "How can you all be here?" I sit up. There is a trembliness to my movements. The end of my leg is wrapped in bandages. The thin sheet covering my body shifts so I can tell something is wrong about the end of my leg but I can't tell exactly what. I suspect whatever is under the bandages is healing messily.

"Your wound was infected," says Nuolo from behind everyone. "I thought it would kill you. We sent for your family. We knew they would want to see you and we needed them to take away the body. That was six days ago. We're all surprised to see you awake now."

Shully puts a hand on the side of my face. "Get some more rest, dear, so we can bring you home."

I lay my head back down. I feel light-headed and disoriented. It is as if the ground is threatening to tilt and spill me out of the cot. It is hot and humid inside the tent. I cling to the blanket.

Luolo brings me a mug of some kind of bitter, lukewarm tea. Still lying down, I awkwardly sip it while I watch Kolb playing with Pixa on the ground. Every couple of minutes, Pixa stops what she is doing to grin goofily at me and wave and say, "Hi, Daddy." Kolb never looks up at me.

Shully sits next to me on the mattress and tells me Kolb has been helping her take care of Pixa. I am relieved to see how well they're getting along, and how little Kolb's wildness is showing through at the moment, but I worry. Sometimes Kolb just wants to destroy things. He could up and run away. He doesn't speak. "What if Pixa stops speaking?" I say, and Shully laughs at me. Pixa, she points out, has been jibber-jabbering to herself the entire time she's been playing, directing Kolb to do one thing, then to do another. Pixa is a talker.

I recognize my problem with Kolb watching Pixa all the time is not anything about Kolb. It is that I want it to be me spending this time with her, playing on the floor and showing her the world is full of small, strange joys.

Instead, I am a living example of how much can go wrong, how much suffering awaits any struggling person who fails to overcome their misfortunes. Being this object lesson for her is what I hate most. But I am helpless to be anything else.

I take another slurp of tea, then hand the mug to Shully. I close my eyes. When I open them, it is night. A cool draft blows through the tent.

My stomach grunts. I'm hungry.

Did my stomach always grunt like that when I was hungry? Does it sound different now? I sit up and pull away the sheet to look at my belly. It just looks like my belly. Remembering the hygienic void makes me want to starve myself, so the thing inside starves. It's not a serious thought. I'm not strong enough to starve myself. But I'm alone and I don't know how I'm supposed to get food. No, I'm not alone: I see the dark shapes of Shully, Kolb, and Pixa sleeping on the floor.

The image of Weckett holding up the void keeps returning to my mind, and with it, waves of nausea. Yet still, somehow, I am hungry.

I lay back down. I'm too hungry to sleep.

I think about deer meat roasted over the fire.

I think about crayfish soup with snails and beans.

I think about dandelion greens fried in oil with garlic.

I think about apples and strawberries and peaches.

I think about bread.

I sit up again, and swing my legs over to the edge of the cot. As quietly as I can, I attempt to hop off to go in search of whatever crumbs I can find.

My good foot hits the floor. I'm fine. I hop on one leg toward the opening of the tent. What time is it? How much time had passed? I have no idea. Maybe if I get past my family without disturbing them, there will be others outside who are still awake. Maybe I'll find Gar or Luolo by the fire. Maybe they'll help me find something to eat.

As I am about to hop out the door, I lose my

balance. I reach out to steady myself on one of the tent's ribs. I miss and I can't stop myself from putting my weight onto my mangled foot.

I scream.

I am falling and reaching all around myself to steady myself and this time my fingers do succeed in grabbing hold of one of the tent's ribs.

But I keep falling. And I keep screaming. I pull down part of the tent with me and land face down on the dirt floor. I hear Shully calling my name.

I look up, confused. I am looking around outside and not understanding what I'm seeing, where I am.

I see we're not at the mold farm worker encampment at all, as I had thought. We are in an open field. Dimming stars dot the blue-black sky. The sun is about to rise. Tents and tables and carts are set up along dirt paths. On the far end of the field, groups of traveling shopkeepers are arriving and spreading themselves out across the field. A conglomerate of the nglaeylyaethm's crystal towers floats obscenely over the scene.

We're at the market.

Shully is yelling at me now, demanding to know if I'm alright, demanding to know what I was thinking, what I was trying to do.

"I'm alright," I say to Shully.

Pixa climbs on top of me and starts hugging me. It's uncomfortable, the way her sharp little knees and elbows dig into my back, but I don't care.

Kolb helps Shully fix the tent. He grunts softly as he puts the ribs back up. When he is finished he looks toward Shully, seeking her approval. She nods and smiles at him.

Shully removes Pixa from me. Together, she and Kolb help me limp back inside. The sun may be rising but my aching body is demanding more sleep. I curl up on the cot and cover myself with blankets and do my best to ignore the sounds of Shully, Kolb, and Pixa beginning their day.

Abruptly, I realize Uli is missing.

Uli is missing and no one is talking about it.

A wave of nausea hits my gut. First I was hungry and now I feel sick. I wonder if the hygienic void feels my pain. I hope so. I sit up and bring my knees to my chest and suck in air between my teeth, hissing.

Shully is at my side. "What's wrong?" she asks.

"Where is Uli?" I ask.

Her empty expression tells me all I need to know.

22

NIGHT.

I crawl on my hands and knees across the market toward Jolm's caravan.

The people Jolm will sell as pets are tied up in bags, drugged and half-asleep. When they become aware of my presence, they mumble among themselves, groggy and suspicious about my intentions.

I take out a knife. The closest person in a bag to me is a balding man with a knotted black beard. He sees me coming toward him with the knife and he says, "No," in a weak, distracted voice, as if his suffering has taught him fighting back is pointless.

I use the knife to cut open the bag and untie ropes that bind him. He spills out of the bag, a mass of filthy limbs on the dirt floor, his face against the ground, weeping.

Then the man stands up and runs away.

I cut free the next would-be pet, and the next. Soon Jolm's caravan is full of men and women standing up and running away from the end they'd resigned themselves to.

Once all the people who had sold themselves into servitude are free, I allow my broken body to collapse on the floor.

I am laughing.

Some of the freed pets pick me up and hoist me onto their shoulders and carry me out of the caravan. Outside, I see they have surrounded the tent where Jolm sleeps.

They are setting Jolm's tent on fire.

The tent burns around Jolm, who is screaming and trying to get away, but every time he gets out of the fire they shove him back in. They keep shoving him back in until he stays in.

The newly freed pets light torches in the fire. They carry me far away until Jolm's burning tent is a distant glowing speck.

They carry me until we reach Weckett's mold farm.

They put me down on the ground. Then they use their torches to set the mold-ridden houses on fire.

The smell is awful.

Mechanoids march to the farm's defence. They are big and slow, and they topple easily when enough people are shoving from one side. Their metal arms and legs are ripped off, and the freed pets use them to smash the mechanoids into little pieces.

Weckett comes out of his crystal cocoon. He has a gun. He starts shooting.

I stand up and once I am standing I find I can keep standing without any assistance or pain.

I charge at Weckett. He shoots at me and misses. I get close enough to grab his gun. I grab it. He doesn't let go. I get one of my legs wrapped up with his legs, tripping him and bringing us both down.

Now I'm on top of him.

Now I have his gun.

Now he's begging for his life.

I shoot him in the face and his face explodes into a mass of tentacles. The tentacles bind my wrists and coil around my throat and with surprising strength pull my head down into the ragged maw that was his face.

23

I WAKE UP ON THE DIRT FLOOR. I'm inside the tent where I've been recovering. I realize I'm thrashing around in the muted sunlight coming through the mask wearer membranes that make up the tent walls. There are hands all over me. I am punching and kicking.

A familiar voice is saying, "Thorner, it's me! Wake up, Thorner! Wake up!" and I gradually become aware that what I am resisting is Shully and Kolb's attempts to lift me back up onto my cot.

I must have fallen onto the ground in the night. I am surprised the fall didn't wake me.

"You have a visitor," Shully is saying. "Someone came to see how you're doing. Someone who has made it possible for you to be here, recovering."

The tent flap opens. Bright sunlight frames the

visitor's silhouette. The visitor comes toward me. She moves stiffly.

Hecla, I think, unable to make out the visitor's features. *She's here to kill me. She's here to do what she said she would do.*

But it's not Hecla.

It's Uli.

I'm relieved.

Now we're all here.

Now we are whole again, a family.

Now, nothing can separate us.

Uli stands at my bedside. She holds the side of my face in her hand. Her eyes dart over my tortured body.

There's something off about the way she looks at me.

I take her arm in my hand.

I pull her close, as if to embrace her.

She resists a little. But she lets me hug her.

My hand moves up from her back to the back of her head.

I feel the cold tentacle buried at the base of her skull.

Uli pulls back.

I turn my head to stare at the mass of tentacles quietly filling the tent entrance behind her.

Her hand takes my chin and guides my gaze back to her face.

In her eyes I can see she is still there.

She is still there, and she is here with me because she wants to be.

And I grudgingly accept her gift of our momentary togetherness and I accept her gift of my recovery and also that I am a gift and also that I must give and give and give of myself as much as I can while I can.

I must keep giving until I am used up, as I know I and everyone around me will be.

Acknowledgments

To all who looked at this furious little book and offered feedback and encouragement, thank you. Special thanks to Nathan Kukulski for his eagle-eyed edits, Brandon Getz for the feedback he provided on an early version of the story, and Brian Evenson for his thoughtful insights and advice. I also want to give a shout out to the Pittsburgh lit scene, the Pittsburgh left scene, and to my all friends and family. I couldn't have done this without you. Solidarity.

RICK CLAYPOOL is the author of the novel *Leech Girl Lives* (Spaceboy Books, 2017). His short fiction appears here and there online and has been anthologized in *The Future Will Be Written by Robots* (Spaceboy Books, 2020) and *Not My President: The Anthology of Dissent* (Thoughtcrime Press, 2018). By day he works for a nonprofit organization researching corporate crime. He spent most of his life in Western Pennsylvania and now lives in Rhode Island, where he goes looking in the woods for fungi as frequently as he can.

www.rickclaypool.org

@weirdstrug on Twitter

CPSIA information can be obtained
at www.ICGtesting.com
Printed in the USA
BVHW030450091220
594999BV00003B/170